THE BEGGAR'S MAGIC

A CHINESE TALE

To Alexandra, Amelia, Celeste, Clare Anne, Daniel,
Jonathan, Matthew, Riley, Wesley, and Zachary
—M.C. and R. C.

Also by Margaret and Raymond Chang:

In the Eye of War

The Cricket Warrior: A Chinese Tale
 illustrated by Warwick Hutton

(Margaret K. McElderry Books)

Margaret K. McElderry Books
An imprint of Simon & Schuster Children's Publishing Division
1230 Avenue of the Americas
New York, New York 10020

Text copyright © 1997 by Margaret and Raymond Chang
Illustrations copyright © 1997 by David Johnson

Book design by Ann Bobco.
The text of this book was set in Perpetua.
The illustrations were rendered in ink and watercolor and colored pencil.

Printed in Hong Kong by South China Printing Co. (1988) Ltd.
First Edition
10 9 8 7 6 5 4 3

Library of Congress Cataloging-in-Publication Data
Chang, Margaret Scrogin.
The beggar's magic : a Chinese tale / retold by Margaret and Raymond Chang ;
illustrated by David Johnson.—1st ed.
p.   cm.
Summary: Retells an ancient Chinese tale of magic in which unselfishness is rewarded.
ISBN 0-689-81340-6
[1. Folklore—China.] I. Johnson, David, 1951-   ill. II. Title.
PZ8.1.C3584Be   1997
398.2'0951'01—dc20
[E]   96-20865   CIP   AC

THE BEGGAR'S MAGIC

A
CHINESE TALE

RETOLD BY

Margaret
&
Raymond Chang

ILLUSTRATED BY

David Johnson

MARGARET K. McELDERRY BOOKS

One day, long ago, a stranger came to a village in China. Fu Nan, who lived with his parents on a farm outside the village, was the first to meet him. He thought the old man looked like a wandering priest, the kind he'd heard of in the old stories. A priest who could work magic. Fu Nan was frightened by his sudden appearance, but the stranger's expression was kind and serene. Fu Nan greeted him politely.

"This looks like a good place to stay for a while," the old man said. "Do you know where I can sleep?"

Fu Nan showed him an abandoned cottage on the outskirts of the village. There the old man made himself a bed of straw and hung up a piece of paper painted with large, rough writing. He called this hut his monastery. Every morning, Fu Nan and his friends would peer through the window, waiting for the old man to wake up.

The children liked to keep the old man company while he begged for food. He was always cheerful, and he never seemed to notice the weather. Rain or shine, the old man wore the same shabby sandals and tattered garment. Since everyone knew that wandering priests took a vow of poverty, the villagers gladly gave the old man rice and vegetables.

Fu Nan warned him not to visit stingy Farmer Wu, the richest man in the district. "He set his dogs on the last beggar who came to his door," Fu Nan said.

Because they were with him so often, the children were the first to discover that the old man had unusual powers.

One morning, when he greeted the children at his door, the old man saw the son of the basket maker holding a sparrow in a cage. The bird fluttered miserably against the bars of its prison.

"Will you let the bird go if I show you a magic trick?" the old man asked him.

Wide-eyed, the boy nodded. The old man went into his hut and returned with a black cloth, an ink stick, paper, and a brush. He draped the black cloth over the cage. The children watched silently as he mixed ink and water. In a few quick strokes, he painted a picture of the caged sparrow. It was so lifelike they thought it might start to sing. He finished by painting the door of the cage standing open.

The painted sparrow twittered and flew out the open door, swooping off the paper and up to the branch of a nearby tree. The basket maker's son snatched away the black cloth that covered his cage. Fu Nan and the others cried out in amazement. The cage was empty.

The priest smiled at the boy. "You have done a kind deed," he said. "You have allowed a wild creature to follow its nature and fly free."

"Can you teach me that trick?" Fu Nan asked the old man later.

The old man spoke gently. "Before I could work this magic, I had to give up all I owned to become a priest. Then I studied for years, and vowed never to use my magic for selfish gain. You're young yet. Wait a while to find your way."

In the village, Fu Nan sometimes helped frail Widow Liang carry heavy buckets of water from the village well to her house, because there was no water left in her well. One hot day, Fu Nan heard the old man ask Widow Liang, "How long has your well been dry?"

"It's been a year since Farmer Wu diverted the stream that fed my well to irrigate his pear orchard," Widow Liang replied.

"Maybe I can help you," the priest said. He poured a dipper full of water down Widow Liang's well. The next morning, she found it brimming with fresh, sweet water.

Fu Nan and Widow Liang were the only witnesses to this marvel, but a few days later the whole village saw the beggar-priest's magic.

On the day of the August Moon Festival, the road to the village was crowded with merchants and farmers carrying their goods to market. Fu Nan's parents set out with baskets of cabbages on their backs. When Fu Nan saw the priest, he asked his parents if he could walk with the old man.

Fu Nan began to tell the old man about the new kite he wanted to buy with his birthday money. Suddenly there was a commotion on the road behind them. Farmer Wu's donkey, pulling a cartload of pears, charged down the crowded road, making everyone scatter. Farmer Wu beat the overburdened donkey, yelling at it to move even faster.

By the time Fu Nan and the old man reached the village square, Farmer Wu was already selling pears from his cart. The hot sun made everyone thirsty, and the sweet, juicy pears sold well, though the farmer demanded a high price.

"May I have one of your luscious pears?" the priest asked Farmer Wu.

"Go away, you ragged beggar! You won't get a handout from me," Farmer Wu shouted.

"But you have so many," the old man pleaded. "Surely you can spare just one."

A crowd gathered to watch the argument. Someone called out, "Don't be so stingy! Give the old man a pear!" But the farmer angrily waved his stick and cursed the priest.

Fu Nan dug into his pocket, trying not to think about the new kite he'd dreamed of buying. The kite can wait, he told himself, and quickly handed his coins to Farmer Wu.

All his birthday money would buy only one small pear. Looking down at the dusty ground so the priest couldn't see how much he had wanted a new kite, Fu Nan held out the pear to him with both hands.

After bowing his thanks, the old man spoke to the people around him. "Because so many of you have shared food with me," he said, "I am going to treat everyone to a delicious pear." He strolled across the village square, and the crowd followed him. Curious as the rest, Farmer Wu followed the crowd.

The priest stopped at the other side of the square and ate the small pear in a few quick bites, until all that remained was one tiny black seed.

The priest pulled a spade from the bag on his back, dug a hole in the dirt, and planted the seed. "Fu Nan," he called, "fetch me a kettle of boiling water."

Fu Nan returned with a kettle from a nearby teashop. The old man poured hot water over the dirt. Instantly a green sprout appeared. Within minutes, the sprout grew into a tree and branched into leaves and blossoms, attracting bees and butterflies. Birds sang from the branches.

The flowers became small green pears that quickly ripened into golden-brown fruit. The old man sniffed a pear. "I think they are ready to eat," he said. Carefully, he picked the pears and offered one to each villager. He gave the largest, ripest pear to Widow Liang.

"Sweet! Juicy! Delicious!" people said, marveling at the priest's magic.

As soon as the last pear had been picked, the leaves turned brown and started to fall. The branches that had looked so strong grew dry and twisted.

"The tree has given up its fruit," the old man said. With his axe, he chopped it down and handed out dry branches to the people for firewood.

He dusted off his hands and rummaged through his bag for a scrap of paper, which he gave to Fu Nan. "When you get back home," he whispered, "tie a string to it, and see what happens."

Then, waving good-bye, the priest walked down the road toward the mountains.

Everyone clustered around, talking about the magic they had seen. Fu Nan put the scrap of paper in his pocket and went to find his parents.

A roar of rage from across the village square stopped Fu Nan. People turned to see Farmer Wu standing near the spot where his cart had been. His pears and cart were gone. Only the cart's wheels and the donkey remained.

Then Fu Nan understood. The old man had conjured away Farmer Wu's pears, and used the cart shaft and body to make the tree.

Farmer Wu also realized what had happened. He ran after the priest, pushing his way across the crowded square, yelling, "Stop that old beggar! He stole my pears!"

But the priest was far away down the road, and behind Farmer Wu the villagers laughed so hard they could barely stand up.

Ever since that day, the story of how Farmer Wu lost his pears has been told as a warning. "Don't be stingy like the foolish farmer, or you'll end up a laughingstock," parents still say to their children.

Ever since that day, the basket maker's son has loved to watch sparrows flying around the village, but he has never caught another bird. Widow Liang's well is always filled with pure water, even in times of drought.

And the scrap of paper the old man had given to Fu Nan turned into a splendid kite. The first time he flew it, on the evening of the August Moon Festival, he knew it was finer and stronger than any kite he'd ever owned. A sudden breeze gusted in the still air, lifting it majestically into the sky. Holding the string and listening to the sound of the kite's tail flapping in the wind, Fu Nan could feel the old man's presence. Someday, he thought, he would be ready to leave the village and follow the old man over the mountains.

AUTHORS' NOTE

"Planting Pears" appears in a collection of tales of magic and the supernatural gathered by Pu Songling (1640-1715) from the people of his native Shandong (Shantung) province. Selections from his book, one of the most popular in China, were first translated into English with the title *Strange Stories from a Chinese Studio* by Herbert A. Giles in 1908. The wandering sage with extraordinary powers appears often in Chinese folklore. Pu Songling calls the conjurer in "Planting Pears" a Taoist priest. These awe-inspiring men were said to study for years to learn their magical powers, including the secret of immortality. Precepts of Taoism were adopted by Chan Buddhists in China and spread to Japan as Zen Buddhism, a philosophy that has influenced twentieth-century Western thought.

Margaret and Raymond Chang